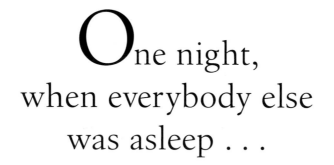

One night,
when everybody else
was asleep . . .

Tom was still awake, reading with his torch.
He had nearly finished his book . . .

when a huge hand tried
to steal his teddy!

The Teddy Robber

Ian Beck

PICTURE CORGI

For Edmund and Laurence
who helped

THE TEDDY ROBBER
A PICTURE CORGI BOOK 978 0 552 55319 3

First published in Great Britain by Doubleday,
an imprint of Random House Children's Publishers UK

Doubleday edition published 1989
Picture Corgi edition published 1991
This Picture Corgi edition published 2006

9 10 8

Picture Corgi Books are published by Random House Children's Publishers UK,
61–63 Uxbridge Road, London W5 5SA,
a division of The Random House Group Ltd.

Addresses for companies within The Random House Group Limited can be found at:
www.randomhouse.co.uk/offices.htm

THE RANDOM HOUSE GROUP Limited Reg. No. 954009
www.randomhousechildrens.co.uk

A CIP catalogue record for this book is available from the British Library.

Printed in China

But Tom wouldn't let go.

Tom's teddy was pulled through the window and thrown into a sack.

Tom tried to hold on, but he slipped down a massive arm, swung on a big iron key . . .

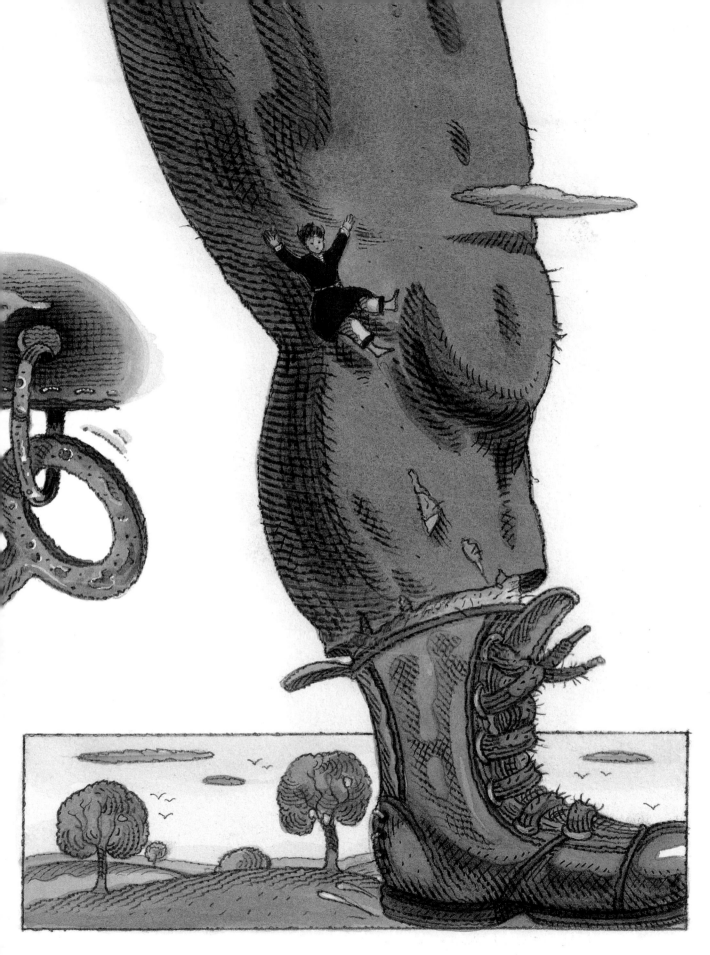

and slithered down a mighty leg.

The Teddy Robber was a GIANT!

Off went the giant with great long strides,
while Tom clung on tight to a bootstrap.

They came to the giant's castle . . .

Tom clambered up the steep steps
after the giant . . .

higher, and higher, and higher,
and higher . . .

until they came to a giant door.

Through the door was a vast room.

Tom climbed up the huge table leg, and saw
the giant with a sack of stolen teddies.

The giant picked up the teddies
one by one.

He looked at each bear *very* carefully.

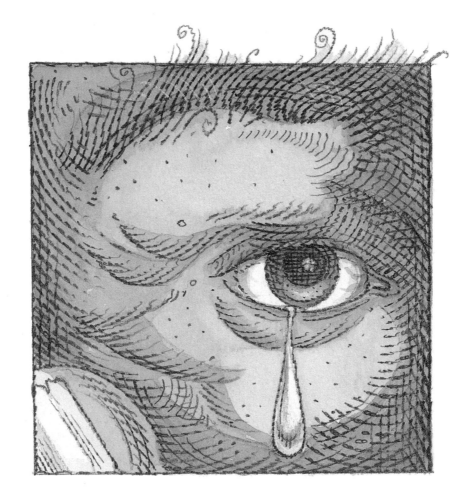

Then the giant sighed a great sigh
and shed a single tear.

He picked up all the teddies
and a big iron key.

He took the key to a huge padlock
on a huge cupboard.

Inside were . . .

all the lost teddies
in the world.

The giant locked the cupboard.
Then he turned round and saw Tom.
"Who are you?" he boomed.
"I'm Tom and you stole my teddy!"

"I've lost my teddy," wailed the giant.
"That's *why* I'm the Teddy Robber."
And he sat down on his bed and sobbed.

"Cheer up," said Tom. "Blow your nose,
and I'll help you look for him."
They looked under the bed.

They looked in
the fridge.

They looked in the
cupboards.

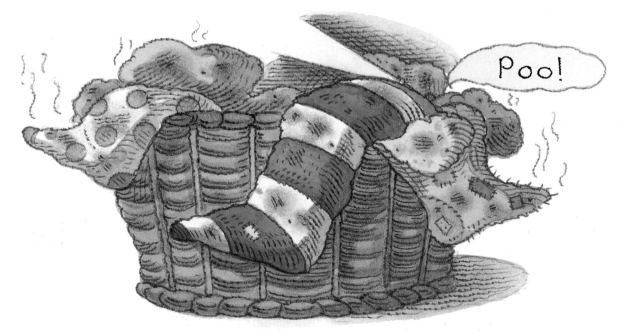

Poo!

They looked in the dirty clothes basket.
They looked everywhere.

"We'll never find him," said the giant, and they
sat down and had a mug of cocoa together.
"Would you like a biscuit?" asked the
giant politely.

"The biscuits are on your pillow," said Tom.
The giant looked surprised.
"They ought to be on the shelf – the pillow
is where my teddy used to be."
And he began to cry all over again.

"If the biscuits are on your pillow," said Tom,
"then perhaps your teddy is . . .

on the shelf!"

"My teddy! My teddy! You've found him!
How can I ever thank you?"

"First you can give me back *my* teddy and
then you must put back all those
stolen teddies – straight away!" said Tom.

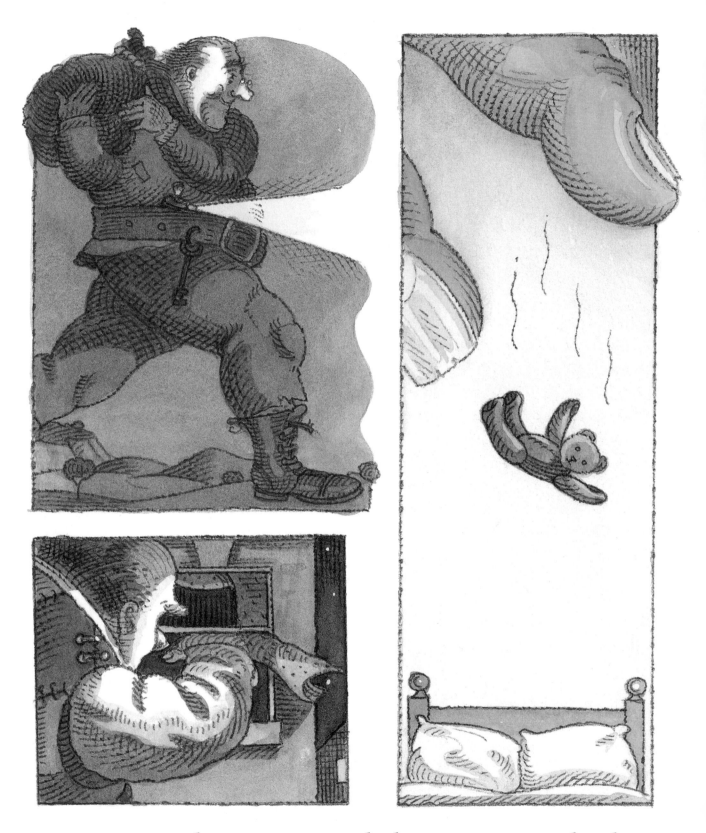

So together Tom and the giant worked
all through the night to put the lost
teddies back in their beds.

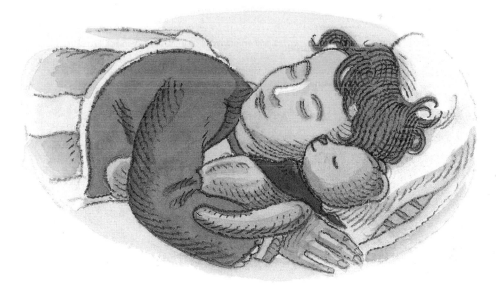

When they had finished, Tom went
safely to bed with his teddy . . .

and the giant cuddled up
with his teddy and was
soon fast asleep.